If It
Bleeds

If It
Bleeds

LINDA L. RICHARDS

RAVEN BOOKS
an imprint of
ORCA BOOK PUBLISHERS

Library and Archives Canada Cataloguing in Publication

Richards, Linda, 1960-, author
If It bleeds / Linda L. Richards.
(Rapid Reads)

Issued also in print and electronic formats.
ISBN 978-1-4598-0734-1 (pbk.).--ISBN 978-1-4598-0735-8 (pdf).--
ISBN 978-1-4598-0736-5 (epub)

I. Title. II. Series: Rapid reads
PS8585.I182513 2014   C813'.54   C2014-901952-1
C2014-901953-X

First published in the United States, 2014
Library of Congress Control Number: 2014936095

Summary: Nicole Charles is a gossip columnist for a big city paper
who gets the chance to cover a murder after she finds the body. (RL 4.0)

*Orca Book Publishers is dedicated to preserving the environment and has
printed this book on Forest Stewardship Council® certified paper.*

Orca Book Publishers gratefully acknowledges the support for
its publishing programs provided by the following agencies:
the Government of Canada through the Canada Book Fund and the
Canada Council for the Arts, and the Province of British Columbia
through the BC Arts Council and the Book Publishing Tax Credit.

Cover design by Jenn Playford
Cover photography by Getty Images

ORCA BOOK PUBLISHERS   ORCA BOOK PUBLISHERS
PO Box 5626, Stn. B   PO Box 468
Victoria, BC Canada   Custer, WA USA
V8R 6S4   98240-0468

www.orcabook.com
Printed and bound in Canada.

17 16 15 14 • 4 3 2 1

"I don't mind a reasonable amount of trouble."

—Dashiell Hammett

ONE

To get ahead in my line, you either get a break, make your own or happen to be in the right place at the right time. I got lucky one night with all three. Too bad that meant someone had to die. I try not to think about that.

My being there had nothing to do with the death of Steve Marsh. He would have died even if I wasn't there. Good thing for me, I was.

When I arrived, I realized he wasn't at the party. Since I hadn't taken his picture that would cause trouble if not corrected. I'd been told.

"But he's not here, darling," Erica West told me when I asked if she'd seen Marsh. As my question sunk in, she arched an eyebrow at me. The lights in the gallery made her pale hair shine. It reflected the dried-blood gloss of her nails.

"He must have been, but I don't see him now," she said. She indicated a back entrance with a rapid flick of her fingers. A waiter caught the motion and rushed over with a tray of drinks. No one denies Erica West. She has a way about her. But she wasn't after a drink. She slid one finger up and down the neck of the ice swan on the table beside her. The motion was innocent enough, yet implied a threat. And not only to the swan.

"I trust we'll see his smiling face in your column in the morning?" she said brightly. Too brightly. I felt a sliver of fear.

I knew I shouldn't reply. I didn't have the right answer. Instead, I asked a question. "What's he drive?"

"Sam can tell you." Another flick of those deadly fingers. This time at a thin man with spiky yellow hair.

"Sam, darling," Erica called, "what does Steve drive?"

"Audi," Sam shot back. "Silver SUV." He barely missed a beat of his chat with three women dressed in black. I grabbed my purse and charged toward the back. Moving in the direction Erica had indicated, I passed through a back room and came out into an alley. It smelled of old brick and rotten garbage.

Vancouver summer days are long. It was after nine at night, and the light was starting to fade. It was going to be a beautiful sunset. At another time, I would have paused to enjoy it. But not tonight. The thought of Erica's perfect nails melting holes in the ice swan's neck floated in my memory like a threat.

The alley was a shock. Inside the gallery, everything was white and clean and the kind of empty that comes with a big price tag. White concrete benches on a polished concrete floor. Hidden lighting. Music floating on clouds.

That gallery could have been on any corner in any good neighborhood in the city. But go out the back door and into the alley, and you remembered it wasn't just anywhere. It was in a part of town that was changing so quickly no one had bothered to tell the whores and the night crawlers.

Patrons of the arts enjoy these dances with the dark side. They think it's cool to have to step over a sleeping drunk or two when they go to a gallery. That way, when they pay big bucks for the work of some artist they've never heard of before, they know they're getting the real deal. It puts them in direct contact with starving for the art. Never mind that most new artists who get those prices for a painting have the support of a good gallery, an arts grant or both.

So the alley was a shock after the clean gallery. A group of junkies saw me come through the door. They began to move my way. Slowly. I didn't think I'd be in danger if they caught up with me. But I didn't feel like getting hassled for spare change. Not in an alley by myself.

I looked down the alley, thinking Steve Marsh would be long gone. Then I could head back into the gallery and nurse my regret with a drink. So I was not happy when I spotted the silver Audi. It was parked a couple of doors down. Idling. Someone in plain sight behind the wheel. I cursed myself. If only I'd tried to answer some of Erica's questions. I'd probably still be in the gallery, and Marsh would have had the chance to drive away.

The junkie pack was closing in on my right. I moved toward the Audi, parked with its taillights facing me. The driver's window was up. Marsh faced away from me. I thought he was maybe talking on the phone. But I couldn't see what he was up to and I couldn't see his face.

I waited, hoping he'd sense me standing next to his car. But he didn't move. And the junkies were closing in. I couldn't just stand there. I raised my hand and tapped on the window. Once, twice, three times. Hard. No response.

By now the whole thing was getting to me. Sure, talk on the phone. Sketch. Whatever. But *move*. Marsh wasn't doing any of that. I could see the freckles on the back of his neck under short dark-red hair. Even in the dim light, I could see the soft fine hairs on his neck. But there was no movement.

And the junkies were getting closer.

I tried the car door. I'd expected it to be locked, but it opened at my touch. Music slid out of the car. The smell of something dark slid out as well. And then, without the support of the door, Marsh began to slide too. I stopped him, pushing him back against the seat. And then I saw.

A short-handled tool was sticking out of the base of his throat. There wasn't a lot of blood. Maybe there hadn't been a great struggle. But somehow I just knew.

I'd never seen a dead person before, but when you see it, you know just what it is.

TWO

I had been covering a gallery opening. That's what my life looks like. When someone in Vancouver puts together some kind of party and they want the press there, they put my name at the top of the list.

It might be to raise money for people left homeless by fire. Or when some politician writes a book. Or a developer has a big new project. Whatever.

A few publicists have told me that when I turn up at one of their events, it's a good sign. "Sure, the snacks were swell," they might say. "And the music was great.

But did Nicole Charles come?" And if I did, everyone is glad. I never get used to that.

Every day, Bryce the mail guy delivers a thick stack of invites to my desk on the fifth floor of the *Vancouver Post* building. I spend an hour or so each day looking through them. Sometimes the mail includes gifts or food, which I don't want and cannot keep.

My email has just as many invitations, though no food or gifts. I notice when I get an email invite followed by a snail-mail invitation followed by still another email. It means they've got the money to be paying for more promotion. Not just the email, which everyone knows is cheap to do.

Lots of invites means the food at the party in question will be good. If you have a big pile of invitations, why not pick the one that's going to have the best food? Most of my fellow journalists would find a lot of things wrong with that, so I don't tell them. I have to pick somehow, don't I?

I have to choose. That seems as good a way as any.

There are times when I have no choice. In those cases, one of my editors or a big shot from the business end will hand me an invitation. "It would be lovely to see you and your camera there, Nicole. I *know* it will be a good party." They say it like it really *is* an invitation. But since they're bosses, they have power over me. I generally put the invitations they hand me near the top of the pile. Then I make sure I go to that party. I go early enough in the evening that everyone isn't drunk. That way I can get photos of all the beautiful people while they're still looking beautiful.

The day of the night Steve Marsh died, Erica West, sales manager, stopped by my desk. She said she was on her way home. Since her office is on the seventh floor and mine is on the fifth, I found it odd.

"Darling Nicole," she said brightly as she popped her head into my cubicle.

"You look *dashing* today. Can a woman be dashing? If she can, then you are."

Dashing. I looked down at myself. Tried to think what I was doing to have earned it. But nothing about my black pants, black blouse or even the black leather jacket slung over the back of my chair seemed dashing to me.

"Uh…thanks, Erica. You look…kinda dashing yourself."

And she did. At five foot five, my height is average. I have brown hair and brown eyes. Fairly average as well.

Erica is not average. She's tall. Close to six feet in the heels she always wears. And she looks even taller when she piles her hair on top of her head, as she had today. She was engaged to the publisher. Not just my boss, but the boss of my whole world. Like a god on his throne up there on the seventh floor in a corner office with a view of the North Shore.

"Darling," the drama queen said. I've never known anyone who can pull off the whole "darling" thing quite like Erica. I thought of her standing in front of a mirror while she practiced saying it. You'd have to, really, to make it come out that smooth.

Erica came closer to my desk. I thought I saw her swallow distaste while she avoided looking at my tiny work space too closely.

She handed me a gold-and-black invitation. It looked expensive. That meant there'd be excellent snacks for sure.

"You've met Steve Marsh," she said.

"No," I said. Erica scares me. She always has. And she's scary, so I've probably got the right idea.

She raised one eyebrow but didn't say anything for a moment. "Hmmmm," she said finally. And then again. "Hmmmm."

"What?" I said, trying to be brave. "I haven't met him. So?"

"His uncle is a friend of mine," she said. "I promised we'd cover his opening."

I stopped myself from asking her what she'd been thinking. After all, she's not my boss. In the newspaper business, the sales department is equal to editorial, not above it. She really had no business even talking to me. She wouldn't, that is, if I was a real reporter, I reminded myself. I'd discovered that the society beat fit somewhere else. I wasn't sure exactly where. But it was clearly below both regular beat reporter and the sales department.

I didn't fool myself. When it came to being a reporter, I was as low as anyone could go and still carry a press pass. I was twenty-seven, not that many years out of journalism school. I had a union job. A lot of my friends were still covering school-board meetings and minor hockey for small papers in small towns. That was *when* they'd been able to find a job.

Even when the news industry is at its best, it's tough to find a job. This wasn't one of those times. I'd been at the right place at the right time and had ended up with my own beat on the largest metro daily west of Toronto. The fact that my beat was easy enough that Bryce the mail guy could have done it was something I tried not to think about. But it was the truth.

There's a rhythm to my job. When someone plans a public event for some company or organization, they hope the news agencies will send a reporter. If they hope it's someone from the *Vancouver Post,* I get sent. I arrive in party clothes with a high-end digital camera so small it fits in my purse.

When the publicist sees me, she puts a drink in my hand. Then she spends way too much energy trying to make sure I have a good time. But I'm not there for a good time, even if I'm partly there for the snacks.

These are not my friends and coworkers. I'm doing my job.

Every event, I try to make sure I get at least one good boob shot. This was not my idea. My predecessor was an old guy. Like a lot of people at our newspaper, he was carried out of the building in a box. Union newspaper jobs are hard to find. No one leaves unless they have to.

It's not like the States, where the next metro daily is just across the street. In Canada, you can count the big papers on both hands. Maybe add in the toes on one foot if you're not too picky.

So the old guy before me blazed the trail. He let the publishing team know that breasts sell newspapers. My column always has to have breasts. Since I tend to cover evening events, they are usually in good supply. Plus, the society women have worked out the whole boobie angle and wave them in my face as soon as I walk in the door. Sometimes it makes me wish I was a guy or a lesbian. All those barely covered boobs are wasted on me. But I know the people reading the paper want to see them, so I get them into as many photos as I can.

It's not just boobs that make my column. I always get at least one hand-some-couple shot. He'll have a strong jaw. She'll have a heart-shaped face. Both of them will have teeth whiter than the paper the picture gets printed on. Of course, any famous people who are there make the cut. People like to see the celebs as much as they apparently need to see boobs.

Some nights, I only have one event to attend. Most of the time, I'm running around town getting to all the events on my list. After my stops have been made and the photos taken, I go home or back to the office and choose which photos will run. Then I write all my clever captions and, if there's room, a witty couple of column inches on each event.

The stars were out tonight! Theater under the stars, that is. Or, at least, anyone who's anyone who works with them. Martinis flowed while maidens delivered angels on horseback. This reporter thought that was an entirely appropriate touch, considering that the first production of the season will be a musical version of Equus. *Elsa Bergermeister glowed in a gown by Vancouver's own Catherine Bert while her daughters, Sara-belle and Jenna-belle, wore Stella McCartney designs selected from the current collection.*

And other stuff like that. None of it high art. None of it what I trained for. None of it doing anything beyond scratching the well-dressed surface.

But then, who trains for this? Does anyone go to journalism school and say,

"When I graduate, I want to be the chick who goes to parties and writes about everyone"? Everyone wants to report crime or war, which, these days, is almost the same. When you study journalism, you want to tame the mean streets. You want to solve the city's problems. To be like a cop with a keyboard and smartphone instead of a gun.

Then life happens. I was lucky. I wanted a byline in the first section. Sure I did. But not enough to kill for it.

Then a dead guy almost fell into my lap. And everything changed.

THREE

I stood there for half a minute, looking at the corpse in Steve Marsh's Audi. Looking at the person that had *been* Steve Marsh until not so long before.

I stood there while I thought about what to do. And then I knew.

I pulled out my phone and looked at the crack zombies still shuffling my way. "Dead guy here," I said in a loud, clear voice. "The cops are on their way."

My words had the desired garlic-like effect, the way the mention of police always does with street people. They scattered.

It would have been funny had I not been so scared. And I *was* scared. As much as I'd ever been.

I could have run into the gallery and gotten help. I *wanted* to. But part of me recognized that bad as this was, it might also be a chance. I dialed Mike Webb, the city editor. I hoped he'd know who I was.

"Mike, this is Nicole Charles. You might not know me, but we met at the Christmas party last year and…"

"Christ, Nic. Sure I know you. Everyone in the city knows you."

I'd forgotten that my picture ran with my column every day. Plus sometimes I ended up in the photos I was supposed to be taking. The third wheel in the handsome-couple shot, for instance. Or standing next to a celebrity at some fundraiser. A local quasi celebrity, a face and name familiar to everyone who read the paper, even if they were never quite sure *why* my mug was known.

"I've got a...I've got a situation here, Mike."

"Where's here?"

"Gallery opening. Downtown Eastside. The artist is dead. I found him. In his car. In the alley."

"Christ," Mike said again, but I could hear him thinking. "So you're on Skid Row with a dead guy. Who else knows?"

"That's why I called. No one knows, Mike. Not yet. I just found him. Like I said, in his car."

"Natural causes?"

I looked at the tool sticking out of Marsh's neck. "I don't think so."

"Okay, let me think. I'll send someone down, but I don't know who's available...maybe Cross, or Hartigan might be around..." I imagined Webb with a chart or computer file, looking for a reporter he could send over.

"That's just it, Mike. I want to cover it."

"I don't know, Nicole…"

"I can do this," I said. "And I'm already here. But I think you should send a photographer. The kind of pictures I take are… well, they're not the same as this."

He kind of laughed, but it wasn't a funny sound. "I get your point. Okay. I'll see what I can do, but you better take what you can, Nicole. Case like this, your next call had better be the cops. I don't imagine they'd want us to camp on a body."

"That's really the reason I called. I wasn't sure if there were rules…"

"Rules? When a reporter finds a stiff? That's not in the book, Nic. We're never there *before* the news happens. Just take the pictures and make the call. Then get back here and we'll get you going on the story."

I knew it wasn't right to smile over a dead man's body, but I couldn't help it. And me not getting the story wouldn't make Steve Marsh any less dead.

So I did what I thought needed to be done. I didn't touch anything, just used my little digital camera to photograph Marsh from a couple of different angles. I did it from outside the car, through the front and side windows. I even zoomed in on the tool sticking out of his neck. Reasoning that no one wants to run a corpse shot on page one, I backed up a few feet and took a picture of the car, Marsh's head just a shadow on the driver's side. And *then* I called 9-1-1.

"I've found a dead man in a car in an alley off Carrall Street."

"Are you sure the man is dead, miss?"

"Quite sure. There is a tool sticking out of his neck."

At the question, I had a sudden doubt and looked back at Marsh. And the doubt was gone.

"Quite sure," I repeated.

There was more. I don't remember the details. I know I gave the address and said I'd stand by, and it seemed as though moments later, the scream of sirens filled the air. Multiple sirens, which surprised me. But then, maybe they didn't get dead bodies called in every day.

The cop behind the wheel of the cruiser had her dark hair pulled back under her hat. Her smile was reassuring and genuine. I figured her to be someone's mom. Her partner was a couple of years younger than me and looked pretty green.

An ambulance and a fire truck arrived at pretty much the same time, but it was clear this was going to be the cops' show.

The woman said she was Sergeant Itani. Her partner was Constable Vickers.

"You found the body? Called it in?"

I just nodded. For once, at a loss for words.

She checked the scene calmly. Marsh was dead. That was easy to see. But I didn't say anything. Itani looked like she knew her job.

"Yup," she said quickly. "Dead." And then to Vickers, "Tell the ambulance. Let them do their stuff."

By now, the alley was more crowded. The meth zombies had moved on, but people from the gallery were beginning to come out to see why the cops were there. Some of them still held drinks. A few lit cigarettes as soon as their lungs hit the night air.

I ignored them all. I was focusing hard on keeping emotional distance from the whole thing. I knew I'd need that if I wanted to cover the artist's death. Reporters aren't meant to be part of the story. And I was aware of that, even while I gave Itani a brief statement. After all, I didn't really know anything.

It wasn't much of a statement. I'd left the gallery at about 9:30, looking for Marsh in order to take his photo for the paper. No, I'd never met him. Yes, I knew what he looked like and I'd been told what he drove. I'd spotted his car up the alley, had gone to it, seen him inside looking none too healthy and called 9-1-1.

It didn't take five minutes. And it was the truth. But somehow it didn't cover it.

The silence I'd felt in the alley, the sense of waiting and—yes—of beauty.

The look of the hair on the back of Marsh's neck.

The smell that had come out of the car with him. Blood. And dying.

The fear I'd had of letting him slide to the ground. It had been as though I needed to keep him in his car at any cost.

And, finally, realizing that someone I had once shared air with did no longer.

I knew that this night had held things I'd always remember. None of that made it into the police report. And I knew none would be in the paper.

It didn't have a place.

FOUR

While I gave my statement, the ambulance guys tried to resuscitate Marsh. I could have told them he was beyond resuscitation, but they didn't ask me.

Once Marsh had been officially pronounced dead, Itani seemed to gather her troops. Constable Vickers trailed behind like a puppy.

I stood in the alley, alone and forgotten for the moment.

I took a deep breath. I knew a page-one story might never drop into my lap again. There were steps I needed to take to ensure I got what I needed to write a kick-ass piece on Steve Marsh's death. I knew that I *knew* what those things were. I am a trained journalist, after all. But now, faced with doing it, it was like I knew nothing at all. I thought about the things I'd learned in school and just drew a scary blank.

I put my hand on the cooling hood of a car that was parked in the alley and stood there, trying to clear my mind. Just as I felt myself begin to relax, I heard my name.

"Nicole." A man's voice. I felt my heart sink when I recognized it.

"Hey, Brent. What are you doing here?" I already knew the answer. Brent Hartigan didn't go anywhere if he wasn't on a story. But if he was here, it meant he was working on *my* story. And *that* meant it wasn't really my story. At least, not all of it. Not anymore.

Another thing about Brent Hartigan: he is beautiful. He looks like an actor playing a hotshot young reporter on a television show where everyone is attractive.

Everything about Brent Hartigan's appearance is classical. His nose is aquiline, his cheekbones are high, his pale blue eyes are exotic. If that weren't enough, he is also tall and broad-shouldered, with the careless look of someone who doesn't have to work very hard to stay in shape.

Right now, Brent's beautiful face looked gently amused at my question. "Webb sent me to help," he said.

Alone, the words were fine. But Brent Hartigan was no boy scout. I knew he'd be no help to me.

I didn't know Brent well. But newsroom stories about him were legendary. The only person Brent ever helped was himself. If I'd doubted those stories before, I didn't now. He really was a hell of a reporter, that much was true. I'd read his stuff. He was good. But he was looking at me the way a cat looks at a piece of lettuce. I wasn't even interesting. And I could see that whatever dreams I had of being a reporter, they weren't shared by Brent.

Did Brent's being there mean that Mike Webb had no faith in me? Or that the story was too big for someone as green as me? Whatever it was, when I saw Brent, I knew exactly what I had to do.

"Great," I said. "Sergeant Itani is in charge." I pointed to where the police officer appeared to be gathering her troops. "You'll want to get the lowdown, I guess."

Brent looked at me closely, the pale blue of his eyes visible in the dim light. If he suspected my motives, I couldn't tell. But why would he? He wouldn't think party girl Nicole was a threat.

"Right," he said. "Good. I'll go talk to her. You stay here—I'll be right back."

I nodded, but he didn't see. He was already charging off toward the sergeant. I headed back inside the gallery.

I didn't have much time. It wouldn't take Brent long to get the little information that was available. My only hope was that Itani would stay too busy to talk to him for a while. That might buy me a little more time.

Inside the gallery, the crowd had thinned, and the people left stood in little clusters. Their voices were low and brittle and frightened. Word of Marsh's death had beat me inside.

Erica spotted me as I came in. Even she looked frightened. "Nicole," she demanded as she came to meet me, "tell me what you saw."

"Not now, Erica. I'm working on the story." She looked as though she might reprimand me. Then thought better of it. "What can I do?" she said, surprising me.

"You've been in here the whole time, talking with people?"

She nodded.

"Did anyone seem odd to you?"

"No." She seemed to think, then said again, "No. The girlfriend..." Her voice trailed off.

"What?"

"Well, I guess I did think it strange that the girlfriend arrived late."

"Which one is she?" I asked.

"Over there." She pointed out a woman in her early thirties, standing apart. The young woman wasn't crying, but she had the air of someone who didn't know what to do with herself.

She should have been beautiful. She had perfect features and figure. She wore good clothes, and she wore them well. But though she was visibly upset, the expression that came most easily to her face was one of dissatisfaction.

"That's Caitlen," Erica told me. "Caitlen Benton-Harris." She looked at me expectantly. When I didn't bite, she prodded. "Her father isn't anyone, but the mother was of the department-store Bentons."

I nodded. That clan I knew. Earlier generations had worked hard to build a little local shop into a big chain. Later generations hadn't done much besides spend the fortune their ancestors had made. The chain was gone now. All that was left was the name.

I approached the woman gently. "Caitlen," I said. "I'm sorry for your loss."

She looked me over. Her face asked how important I was. Not at all, it replied a single beat later.

"Thank you," she said nicely enough, though she didn't offer me her hand.

"I'm Nicole Charles," I told her. "With the *Vancouver Post*."

"I know who you are," she said coldly.

"Someone said you arrived late tonight." As I said the words, I could feel what they might imply. Her face confirmed my fear.

"Excuse me?" she said sharply. The people nearest us turned at the sound. I fought the urge to melt into the concrete floor. This was what it meant to be a reporter, I told myself firmly. This was what I needed to do if I was going to get even a toehold in the story. I must ask the hard questions, even if it would be easier not to.

"The police are bound to ask," I said quietly, stating the obvious. "I thought I'd head them off."

"You people make me *sick*," she said with venom. "You're like vultures. You're already here. Circling."

"I found him," I pointed out. "I was here. At the opening. You were not," I pressed. "Where were you?"

"I can't believe this," she cried. "I told you..."

I just looked at her. She hadn't told me anything.

"I told you...I don't have anything to say." It didn't surprise me when she turned away. But when she kept going and left the gallery, I was surprised. Not only that she'd left, but that she'd been allowed to leave. I looked around quickly. The cops weren't inside yet. Someone would want to speak with Caitlen. But would they know to look for her?

I watched her go. There was nothing in her leaving I could write about. Not yet. But I'd remember her actions. If I played my cards right and kept one step ahead of Brent Hartigan, and if I showed Mike Webb I had what it took to do a story this big, I'd be writing about Steve Marsh's death for a long time. Maybe months.

I didn't have experience covering a murder, but I had a feeling. This was a story that would be retold many ways.

FIVE

s I've said, my office is on the fifth floor of the *Vancouver Post* building at the edge of the sea in downtown Vancouver. Even so, when I got back to the building around eleven that night, I had the elevator stop at the fourth floor.

The parking level had been deserted, as had the big marble-floored foyer when I'd swapped elevators to get up to the office level. I knew that had I gone to the fifth level, things would have been quiet there too. Some cleaning crew shuffling through their late-night labors. Maybe not even that.

On the fourth floor, things were different. The doors opened right onto the newsroom, and though it wasn't as hectic as it would have been during the day, the news doesn't stop at quitting time.

The noise level was less low. Still, it was an assault to my senses. When he looked up from his computer at the center of the bullpen, Mike Webb seemed surprised to see me.

"Nicole Charles," I reminded him tentatively.

He grinned. "Stop telling me," he said. "We did that already."

"I know, but that was on the phone...I thought maybe in person..."

"I'm a newsman, Nic," he said with a scowl. "It's my job to know who everyone is."

"Okay," I said, regarding him seriously.

His wide face broke into a grin, and he shook his head. "I'm *kidding*, Nicole.

I'm sorry. It's late. We get a little punchy around here on deadline. I know a lot of people, but I don't know *everyone*. But I do know you. What I don't know is what you're doing here. I sent Hartigan down."

"Yes, sir. I know. I saw Brent there. It's just that…well, I'd hoped that since I was the one that found the body, it could be my story."

Mike looked at me thoughtfully. "You said something like that on the phone."

I knew I wasn't likely to get much of an opening, so I took the teeny one I saw. "I realize you don't think of me as a reporter, Mr. Webb."

"Mike," he corrected. "And please don't call me 'sir' again. It makes me feel like your dad."

"Mike. Okay. But I *am* a reporter. That's what I trained to do."

"How'd you get stuck there then?" he asked pleasantly. I realized it wasn't an insult, just what he saw as the natural order of things. There are news people. Then there are feature writers. Then there's me.

"I did my practicum under Philby Donner," I said.

Mike nodded. "Homes section, right?" And, to his credit, he didn't say it with a sneer. There were others who wouldn't have been as generous. And we both knew why. A lot of real-estate reporting isn't much more than advertorial, covering this new condo development and that new home-care product. There might be the hint of hard news here and there, but you really have to dig to find it.

"Right," I agreed. "Then Howard Enders died during my last week, and…"

"There you were."

I shrugged. That was pretty much how it had gone. What I didn't need to say was that we both knew a green reporter fresh off her practicum after attending a community college would come cheaper than either a seasoned reporter or someone from a better school with hotter prospects. And in the newspaper business, the bottom line is never far from sight. They hadn't looked far to fill Howard's post because they hadn't needed to. I'd been sitting right there, not looking like I'd cause any trouble. And not expecting a hefty paycheck. At least, not right away.

Webb kicked back in his seat and looked up at me thoughtfully. He didn't speak right off. He considered his words. "What you're *really* saying is that you have no reporting experience. That you did the program at… where did you say you went to school?"

I hadn't said. "Delta College."

He'd know the program—it was right outside the city. He'd probably even speak to a grad class every year or so. I couldn't imagine he'd hire anyone for his newsroom straight out of the program though.

Not with his pick of graduates from four-year programs across the country each and every year.

"Nicole...sit down, will you?"

I perched nervously on the chair near his desk. I wasn't sure I liked the way this was going.

"Look," he said, "from what you told me, this may well end up being one of our top stories of the year. Of the *year*. Now, I respect why you feel it's your story. You found the guy. On your watch—you were covering his event, right? But there's no way I can turn you loose on this one by yourself. You're just too green. Hell, you're not *even* green. You've never actually worked on a real murder case, am I right?"

I managed a sort of nod/shrug. I would have liked to deny it, but what he said was true.

"Now, Hartigan has contacts in all the right places. You know yourself, Nicole.

You need those on any story. You wouldn't even know where to start on this one—"

"Oh, but I would," I broke in before he could finish his thought. "I have, even. That's why I came straight in. I have some very strong stuff, Mike. I spoke with…with sources before I left the scene. I'm here to start right on it." I told myself it was not a lie. And I didn't think I'd get a second chance. "I thought you'd want something for the morning edition."

He grinned at me again. I liked the way that grin warmed his face. "You're keen, I can see that. Hungry. That's a good thing. You're not planning on staying in the party room forever?"

"I want to be a reporter, Mike. A real one. The job came up and I've been doing it. I'm even good at it, I think. But I want to be a reporter. That's all I ever really wanted."

He sighed and slumped back in his seat. "You're a smart kid. I can see that. A nice one too. You know I can't give you this story." I started to protest, but he stopped me. "Not all of it. If it was something smaller, maybe, but...well, it's not. Like I said, considering who this guy was and how he died, this might be one of our top stories of the year. I've already got Brent on it, but I think it might be enough story for both of you."

"He won't like that."

Mike grinned again. "You're right about that, but he's a pro. He'll do what I say."

I smiled back at him, but I wasn't so sure.

"How should I...that is...how do you see it working?"

"You write something. He'll write something. You guys talk in between. It'll all work out. You'll see." I must have looked doubtful, because he said it again. "You guys will work it out." It was more order than observation.

I might have said more—I could feel the words forming even as Mike was finishing speaking—but the elevator doors opened with an efficient *swoosh* and Brent Hartigan breezed into the newsroom. It was just after midnight, and he looked as bright and fresh as a Christmas tree on the first of December.

SIX

"Where'd you get to?" Hartigan asked as he walked past Mike's desk. He didn't look surprised to see me. I was surprised at how unsurprised he was.

"I thought I'd get back here and start on the story." I looked straight into his eyes as I said this. Laying it down while the editor looked on. *Our* editor, I corrected myself.

My raised hackles didn't seem to raise Hartigan's at all, which annoyed me. It wasn't that I *wanted* to annoy him. More like I wanted him to see me as enough of a threat that he'd be a little annoyed.

But he looked at me mildly. Even smiled lazily. "Well, good then," was all he said. "That's just fine. And what have you done so far?"

I was aware of Mike Webb watching us from his desk. I didn't know the editor well enough to tell if he was amused or alarmed. In either case, I had a sense Mike wasn't about to intervene.

"Well..." I said, trying to think of a good answer. Coming up short. "Well... nothing, I guess. Not yet. Not so far. Mr. Webb—"

"Mike," he piped up from his desk.

"Mike was just telling me how he thought he saw this going."

"Ah," Hartigan said, more interested now. But only slightly. "And how was that?"

He sat on the edge of Mike's desk, supporting his weight on his heels. I waited for Webb to object, but he didn't. And that action—a single bum on just one desk—did exactly what I guessed Hartigan had meant for it to do. It put me, the little girl who had lost her way back to Features, in her place.

I hiked up my courage. While I did, I saw myself as I'd been in journalism school. The bright kid who'd known she was destined to help make the world a better place.

Oh, sure. I had *a way with words*. I was *good with people*. But there was more to it than that. I had attacked my classes like someone who was hungry for each new assignment. No weekend keggers, trips to music festivals or skiing at Whistler. No hours lost on the beach or rollerblading the seawall. I'd used all my time to study and read and work. In short blocks of free time, I'd dreamed about what my life would be like, the reporter I would be. The difference I would make.

None of it had come true. Things had happened in a way that my working-class upbringing made it difficult to fight. I'd skipped a few rungs on the job ladder. Gone from student to full-time reporter with her own beat. For someone of my age and experience level, the money was good. The money was *real*. Enough to allow me to buy a little car when I first started and some decent furniture and good clothes not long after. Hell, a couple of years later and here I was, the only one of my graduating class with an RRSP.

And I didn't hate the work. Sometimes it was even fun, and the food was great. I barely had to buy groceries. But standing here, with Brent Hartigan appraising me and finding me wanting, it all came back. All the dreams and desires I'd wanted so badly just a few years before. I'd never forgotten. And now it was back.

"Here's how," I said, my confidence real. "You are the senior reporter on this story." I smiled at him sweetly. "But it *is* my story.

You wouldn't have it at all if not for me. I have angles I wish to follow." I saw his bent eyebrow. Ignored it. Went on. "And you likely do as well. We'll set a time to meet before deadline. We'll look over each other's stories, edit what's duplicated, then file it with Mike. He'll run what he needs under our own bylines or with 'files by' bylines if that better describes it." I'd been talking to Brent, but now I looked directly at Mike. "Sound okay?" I asked him, holding on to each shred of confidence for all it was worth.

Mike grinned. I was beginning to realize it was his usual expression. "Sounds good. Let's call it a plan and be prepared to alter it as we go. We good?"

Brent and I both nodded.

"Okay then," Mike said. "Because Nicole isn't based in the newsroom, we have a bit of a logistics problem. Scott is away all month. Nicole, I don't see any reason you can't do most of your writing at your desk on the fifth floor. But if you'd rather work here some of the time, or even just when you and Brent need to be in the same space, use Scott's desk." He looked us over like he might add something, then changed his mind. "All right, you two," he said. "That covers it. And if we're gonna get anything about Marsh into the morning edition, you guys will need to get to it."

I knew there was probably more I needed to work out with Brent, but I didn't know the ways of the newsroom well enough to even start figuring out what they were.

He caught me while I waited for the elevator.

"Goin' home?" he asked. It wasn't a sneer, but it was close.

I smiled sweetly. "More or less. I'm heading to Features. I *will* use Scott's desk, but not tonight. I'll work better in the space I'm used to writing in."

"Is that what you do there?" Brent asked, deadpan.

The elevator came and I walked into it as coolly as possible, not answering him as the doors shut behind me.

"Prick," I said aloud as the elevator got moving.

"Asshole," I said to the empty corridor as I walked to my cubicle. And, potty mouth aside, his words, so mildly applied, had hurt. I mean, obviously, I wasn't going to be nominated for any awards writing about society debs and corporate geezers. Just because the writing I did that appeared in the paper was inane and largely just captions for the photos I took, it didn't mean I couldn't write. I could. I hesitated. Then I corrected myself. I *used* to be able to write. It was so long since I'd done anything like report an actual story that I hoped I still could.

The first few minutes at my desk didn't help. The same insecurity that had stolen my words for a while at the crime scene came back and stole them again. I kept second-guessing myself.

How should a story start? Where was the line that would sum up the whole piece in twenty words or less? What did readers most need to know about the death of Steve Marsh?

I got up and grabbed a copy of the previous day's edition, scanning opening paragraphs frantically, trying to size up the perfect hook. What made this one better than that one? What made that one work where this one did not?

A man charged with the brutal slaying of women near the Commercial Drive SkyTrain station is being held by Vancouver Police though he has not yet been charged with a crime, the Vancouver Post *has learned.*

Too much, I thought. Too many thoughts. Too much qualifying by stating the obvious.

Emboldened by the ability to formulate a critique, I pressed on.

Another story.

Vancouver mayoral contender Campbell Baron is breaking new political ground in B.C. by raising his own money to finance political polling and hire a political staff.

Lots of redundancy, and I wasn't sure anyone would think that using your own money was actual news. Lesson one from journalism school—or perhaps lesson sixteen, but something near the beginning: saying something is does not make it so.

I moved on.

The Conservative government revealed Thursday that former Liberal MP Brewer Hudson spent almost $20,000 in public funds on a trip to Sri Lanka this fall to write a report for Prime Minister Theroux that is now being kept secret.

Some of the grammar wasn't even good here, making me wonder about reporters or editors or both. That, along with the critiques I'd given the others, gave me the confidence I needed. The reporters who had written those stories weren't necessarily better than me, especially not just because they had desks one floor down. They were human and flawed. And since I was also human and flawed, I had a shot. I put the newspaper aside and settled in to write.

The Vancouver art world was shocked last night at the unexpected death of Steve Marsh.

I winced a bit at that "unexpected." Also, the line implied that it wasn't due to foul play. I left what I'd written, but spaced down a few inches and started again.

Prominent Vancouver artist Steve Marsh was found murdered in his car last night outside a gallery that had just opened an exhibition of his work.

That was closer. But not quite.

A few more inches down.

Steve Marsh, a prominent Vancouver artist as well as a member of the Point Grey Marsh family, was found murdered last night outside a Vancouver art gallery.

That was just plain stinky. Again.

Vancouver artist and man about town Steve Marsh was found dead last night outside the downtown gallery that had just opened an exhibit of his work. Foul play is suspected.

That was it. I wasn't nuts about the whole man-about-town thing. But it did imply what I didn't dare say: spoiled dilettante son of a prominent local family.

I forged on, incorporating what I *did* know. A little background and how Marsh fit into the city. The fact that the show had just opened, and what Marsh's place in the Canadian art community had been. The fact that he'd been found dead in his SUV. It was important for readers to have that detail so they could build the right picture. The fact that he'd been found in an alley behind the gallery, while inside admirers were toasting his work. I added some—but not all—of the color I'd experienced. The summer night, the austere air in the gallery once Marsh's death had become known. I dithered awhile about whether I should include my part in it, the fact that I'd found the body. In the end, I decided it wasn't important. Including that detail might cloud the issue and bring my objectivity into question. There were times when knowing I'd been there would have been important, but my part in the discovery had been small. Mike Webb would be my net with this. If he decided it needed to be mentioned, he'd tell me so.

I read it over a thirtieth time and decided I liked what I'd written. It was a good opening piece. I knew this story would continue for days and even months, depending on what the police investigation turned up. There'd be plenty of time to get more background and fill in the details as the story unfolded. My training told me the bare facts were what was needed for this first piece.

With the story written, I connected my camera to my computer and uploaded the photos I'd taken. I chose the best four and emailed them to Mike. Then I gave my story a last once-over, changing a comma here, a word there, and emailed that to Mike as well. I checked my watch. It was 1:15. I was pleased with myself. I'd turned the story around in a couple of hours. I'd head to the news floor and check in with Mike, then home to get some sleep and be back early to get a big start on a follow-up piece in the morning.

When I got there, the news floor was as deserted as I imagined it could ever be. Neither Mike nor Brent was there, and the two reporters I saw just looked at me glassily when I interrupted their typing to ask where either might be.

I felt a tremor of doubt when Mike and Brent weren't around, but only a tremor. I quelled the small voices. It was late. They might have gone for coffee or a bite, together or not. I left a note at Mike's desk, letting him know about the email. Then I left. I was tired, and tomorrow was coming at me so fast it was already there.

SEVEN

I'm lucky. I always have been. Things fall into place. When graduation was near and I needed a job, one came. When the job turned out to be in downtown Vancouver, my family came through with my late aunt's apartment.

It was a tiny apartment in a co-op building off South Granville Street. I was surrounded on two sides by widows who'd been living in the building "since Trudeau was that exciting young man at 24 Sussex," as one of them put it. This was Mrs. Noble, a woman so old I found it difficult to see the young woman she might have been. The fact that she'd been living in the building for over forty years gave me a clue to her age. I knew she'd had a life before that. She talked about it sometimes. A house in Kerrisdale. Kids, a dog—a husband, I presumed, though Mr. Noble was never mentioned and the kids never came by.

On my other side was Mrs. Fast. "Call me Rachel, dear."

Rachel's hair was not blue. It was a rich, dark blond, and though I strongly suspected the color was not her natural shade, I never saw a paler root or a hint of brass. Whoever did Rachel's hair did a good job.

Rachel Fast was a more recent occupant. She told me that when she moved into the building, my aunt Agnes had already secured her end-unit apartment. I knew Agnes had been keeping an apartment in the city since her engineer husband did well in the Alberta oil fields in the late 1970s. It afforded her more than enough money to escape the Edmonton winters and spend time with her brother's family in Vancouver while keeping her own space. It all meant that Rachel had moved into the building more recently than Mrs. Noble, but she still might have been there a quarter century.

There were four apartments to a floor. Two two-bedroom suites—and Mrs. Fast and Mrs. Noble each had one of those—and two very small apartments, mine and another across the hall that was owned by a dentist from Victoria, who we never saw.

I made my way up the stairs to the third floor of the four-story building. I didn't see anyone, nor did I expect to. This late at night, it was unlikely anyone else would be stirring, the Mesdames Fast and Noble firmly tucked away in their beds.

I didn't realize how tired I was until I closed the apartment door behind me and dropped my bags on the table in the small foyer. I aimed to hang my jacket on a hook in the foyer and didn't notice I'd missed altogether until I heard the leather hit the hardwood. I was too tired to pick it up. Too tired to care.

My kitchen is tiny. All sunny yellow tile and ancient appliances. I put the kettle on to boil, then perched at the counter, too keyed up to do anything but make tea.

Something was bothering me. I am no kind of mechanic. And I'm not an expert on tools. But the one sticking out of Marsh's neck had been odd. And not just because it was stuck in his neck.

I grabbed my camera and scrolled to the photos I'd taken of Marsh in his SUV. When I found what I was looking for, I enlarged the image until the handle of the tool filled the entire frame. Then I could see it. The thing that had been bugging me. Though I couldn't see the part buried inside Marsh, the tool was unlike anything I'd ever seen.

It looked like the handle had been turned on a lathe. It was fine work. And it was old. And worn. I sat back and sipped my tea. It made no sense to me, but a picture doesn't lie. The murder weapon was an antique. Perhaps even distinctive and of value. I didn't know what that meant.

I was bone-tired, but I dragged out my computer and checked Google. I couldn't find anything about Steve Marsh that connected him with antiques. In fact, his art had been opposite. It was new and vibrant and modern. Nothing old about it. I dug further.

Family connections. As far as I could tell, no one in his family collected antiques. There were too many Marsh mentions to sort them out, though after a while I got the idea that the wealth of the prominent and proper family had come from questionable sources. That wasn't unique. But the Marshes' connections were more colorful than most. There were hints of rum-running during Prohibition in the 1920s. Canadian rye whiskey, probably acquired through legal sources in Canada, shipped by boat to the United States at great risk and for great profits. But that was long ago. I did the math. Three generations? These present Marshes probably had no recollection of anything beyond private schools and exclusive clubs. I shut my computer. It was interesting stuff, sure. But all it was doing was keeping me awake.

When I went to bed, I was afraid I'd never get it all out of my head. But I was wrong. I was so tired that as soon as my head hit the pillow, there was just nothing at all.

EIGHT

In the morning I got up earlier than usual, wiping sleep out of my eyes. Somewhere nearby there was a coffee with my name on it. More important, there was a newspaper with my name on it, not *in* it as was usually the case. I couldn't wait to get out of bed so I could see my first-ever page-one byline.

Since I have the society beat, I end up working most nights. No one expects me to show up at the office until late in the day. Sometimes I wondered if anyone would notice if I didn't show up at all. If I just filed my stories via email. I wondered, but I'd never tested the theory.

Since no one was expecting me— perhaps *ever*—even though it was nine in the morning on a weekday, I pulled on my running gear and charged out the door.

I ran down Fir Street toward the seawall, then pounded past Granville Island Market and around the island, slowing only for the last half kilometer before I got to Starbucks for my mocha. I grabbed a paper while I waited for my coffee, but I didn't even look at it until I'd sat down and had my coffee and a pastry in hand. I knew this was a moment I wanted to remember. I took a sip of my coffee and forced a bite of my pastry before I spread the paper in front of me.

The story was there, of course. Right on the front page, just as I'd known it would be. One of my photos was there too. But it wasn't my story. Not even a bit of it. And under my photo, it said *Vancouver Post staff* where my name should have been.

Brent's name was there. Of course. And as I read the words under his byline, my disappointment grew into something more dark.

Man about town Steve Marsh was found dead last night outside the downtown gallery that had just opened an exhibit of the artist's work. The Vancouver art community is reeling under the loss of one of its bright young stars.

I'd never been one of Brent Hartigan's biggest fans. I didn't know him well, but there were things about him I'd never really liked. Ambition does alienates people sometimes. I could live with that, especially since I didn't have to live with it.

But this? This was different. As I read I felt something bend inside me. And then I felt it snap.

NINE

Mike Webb had the good grace to look sheepish when I barged into the office an hour later. He also had the good grace to look as though he wished he could melt through the floor rather than meet my wrath. I was glad, somehow. It would have been worse if he just didn't care.

"Nicole," he said. Nothing else. Just my name, as though it were a greeting, or perhaps an explanation.

I didn't say anything at first. Just stood next to his desk, not even noticing when I crossed my arms in front of me as I looked down at him.

"Nicole," he said again, filling the silence he might have thought would be filled with my shrieks. When I didn't shriek, he forced himself to cough up more words. "Look, Nicole, I know what we talked about"— he said it as though I'd filled in words of protest—"but it was a last-minute judgment call. Eleventh hour, really." He finished with a smile, as though he'd lulled himself into thinking my silence was agreement. His body language told me he knew better.

"Whose judgment?" They were the first words I'd spoken.

He coughed, but it was answer enough.

"I understand, Mike." I was pleased that my voice didn't betray much of what I was feeling. I sounded calm. "Maybe I shouldn't, but I do. I don't get the photo though. It *is* my photo, obviously. So I would have expected it to have my byline."

"Me too," Mike said. "I don't know how that happened."

I hesitated a moment before saying what was on my mind. "But my piece? My lede?" I said, using the industry name for an opening paragraph. "You know how *that* happened?"

"Look, Nicole, it was a straight-up news decision. Hartigan looked stuff over last night and—"

"Hartigan did? I sent it to you."

"I was busy. I had other stories. I put Hartigan on it." Mike shrugged. "He made the call, Nic. And I'll back him on it." The jovial face was gone now. You don't get to be a city editor without knowing how to be tough when you need to.

There were things I could have said to Mike. Points I could have made. But none of it would have helped me get where I wanted to go. I opted instead to go forward. There didn't seem to be much point in anything else.

"So what now?" I said calmly.

"Now?" he repeated.

"My story," I said, trying hard to keep my voice from sounding small.

Mike sighed. Rubbed his head. "It's not your story anymore. I'm sorry," he said again. I could tell he was. I could also tell that right then, there was nothing I could do to change his mind. Not stamping my feet, not shouting, not screeching. Not even reminding him what he'd said the night before. So I resisted all those urges. I didn't trust myself to say anything. I just nodded at him. Even tried for a smile and headed for the elevator, my dignity in tatters.

Back on the fifth floor, I forced thoughts of Steve Marsh's death aside. I sorted through the day's stack of invites and firmed up the schedule for the coming evening.

There were two must-attend events downtown. A society benefit at a big hotel and a music launch at a club on Granville. Then, closer to home for me, there was a book launch at a restaurant in Kitsilano, after which I planned to head home and drop my car off before going to a gallery opening in my neighborhood on South Granville. It was going to be a busy Thursday night.

Reading invitations and making notes and even doing online searches on a couple of the celebs expected at that night's events had taken me completely out of my bad mood about losing the Marsh story.

And then the phone rang.

"This is Nicole," I said absently, still focused on my schedule.

"Hello, Ms. Charles." The voice was female and clipped, as though the speaker was in a hurry. It wasn't a voice I recognized.

"Nicole, please." I corrected her automatically.

"Nicole, this is Sergeant Itani, from the Vancouver City Police. We met last night?"

"I remember. Of course."

"Ms.—Nicole, I know you're working on the Steve Marsh story." I thought about correcting her, but I did not. "We've found something. Something I think you should see. Can you be here within the hour?"

I told her I'd be there in fifteen.

TEN

I was so new to the police beat, I didn't even know where "here" was. I had to look it up on my phone.

Vancouver's police HQ was a new glass tower at the foot of the Cambie Street Bridge. It was bland enough to be almost invisible amid the condos that had sprung up around it. A crisp pale cube in a sea of crisp black cubes. I drove past it on my first approach.

Sergeant Itani's office was on the fourth floor. A receptionist buzzed the sergeant when I asked for her. I passed the time in the waiting area pacing mildly.

In uniform but without her police hat and with her hair loose around her shoulders, Sergeant Itani looked younger and friendlier than she had the night before.

"Nicole," she said when she saw me, "thanks for coming so quickly. I appreciate it." I followed her past modern, functional offices. She stopped at one of these. There were no personal touches—no family photos or funny coffee mugs, no clipboards with cartoons or funny sayings. I gathered this wasn't Itani's personal office. Maybe a shared space that field officers used when they had business at HQ.

She closed the door behind us, then sat at the desk and asked me to sit.

"Listen, Sergeant Itani—"

But it was her turn to interrupt. "Rosa, please."

I smiled, then went on. "Okay, Rosa. I feel as though I should tell you...that is, I don't *want* to tell you, but I should..."

"You're off the story, aren't you?" she said calmly.

I looked at her and nodded. I couldn't have been more surprised.

"Thought as much," she said. Where I was surprised, she was not, which surprised me even more. "But let me ask you this— did you *want* to be taken off the story?"

I shook my head and she smiled, looking pleased with herself. "That's what I thought. Listen, between you and me..." She shot a look at the door and, satisfied it was shut tight, went on. "Your Brent Hartigan is a pain in the ass."

I was surprised at her words, but not so surprised that I didn't have a reply. "He's not *my* Brent Hartigan."

She nodded. "That's what I thought. He's a hotshot. The last thing I need on this case is a hotshot getting in the way. Now you"—she stretched back in the chair— "you're controllable."

"Thanks," I said.

She smiled. "Well, it's true, Nicole. You are. And you're green and hungry and you need friends."

My mind was reeling. I wanted to ask her how she knew I was hungry. Was it something anyone could see? I didn't ask. I kept my mouth shut. She had more to say.

She reached into the desk. Drew out a large envelope. Not thick. Slid it across the desk to me, an expectant look in her eyes.

I opened it. The only thing inside was an eight-by-ten photo. I could tell exactly how big the subject was because it had been photographed next to a ruler. It was a good photograph. The kind they take of products in magazines. The kind they take of corpses.

The photo was of a tool, six inches long. It had a handle, like a screwdriver, made of wood. It was red, but the paint had faded, through use or age or a combination of both.

The other end—the business end—was a spike with a hook so slight, you told yourself at first it was an optical illusion. The spike was sharp. And the tool was thicker than a meat skewer, and too short to do that job, but you knew you'd have no trouble stabbing a roast with it.

"You recognize it?" Rosa asked when I'd studied the photo for a moment.

"Of course," I said. "But I don't know what it is."

"It's an antique," she said.

"What's it for?"

"We're not sure. Some sort of tool. Possibly for fishing."

"Why are you showing me?"

"Well, it's the murder weapon—you'll have figured that out already." I nodded and she went on. "And its use in that context seems…pointed."

My eyes widened at the words. It was really a very bad joke, which is what I said. "That's a bad pun."

"Is it?" She looked honestly confused. "Oh. Right. Sorry. That's not what I meant. What I should have said is…it's an odd weapon. An antique awl. Why?" She hooked the photo with her index finger, turned it around, studied it briefly and then spun it back to face me. "Why would anyone use such a thing to kill a man unless they were trying to say something. See what I mean? Unless they were trying to make a point."

"I still don't understand why you're telling me," I said, not commenting on the second bad pun. From the look on her face, she didn't even know she'd made it. "And if I can be perfectly honest? This seems like the sort of detail police would *avoid* giving to reporters."

She smiled. "You watch too much TV."

"Still," I insisted, "*you're* making a point of telling me this. You brought me all the way down here to see the photo. Next you're going to tell me you want me to let people know about it." Maybe I was new to the world of crime reporting, but I could see where this was leading.

She nodded. "Well, you're half right. I'm going to give you this photo when you leave today, but before you go, I'll have your word that you won't use it for three days."

"Three days? Why? And in that case, why give it to me now?"

"We're working the case now. Trying to figure out who did this. Between you and me, doors are slamming shut as soon as we think we're opening them. So you now have this info no one outside this building is aware of. I figure you're going to take this photo with you and not publish it, but keep it in your mind. If none of us have anything solid after three days, the photo of the murder weapon in the paper might grab someone's attention."

"And Hartigan?"

"Ah, Hartigan. He's grandstanded on me on a couple of cases in the past. I wouldn't mind seeing him taken down a bit. I figure you might be the one to do it."

I let all this sink in. It was hard, because I knew there was more going on than I was seeing. On the one hand, Rosa Itani had given me inside information. Stuff I knew Brent wouldn't have access to. It would mean I'd be back on the story in three days at the most. Less if I managed to discover something on my own.

Whatever was going on, I'd gotten all the information out of the homicide detective I was going to get. She was pleasant, but I could tell she wasn't going to say anything more. Either she was using me or I was being given some sort of test. Or both.

I agreed to what she'd asked. I promised I wouldn't publish the photo for three days. Then I picked up the envelope and left.

ELEVEN

In the police parking lot, I got back into my car and headed out with no clear idea where I was going. I had a lot on my mind.

Three days. And since I wasn't even officially *on* the Marsh story, I'd have to be creative and stealthy.

By now the west side was well behind me. I'd picked the twisty road that followed the river out of Vancouver and into Burnaby. I couldn't deny where I was going any longer. I was on my way to see my mom.

My family home is on Capitol Hill, which is a lot less posh than it sounds.

It might once have been a posh neighborhood, but by the time my parents bought the house in the mid-1970s, it was filling up with immigrant families, like ours.

Our house has a gorgeous view toward South Burnaby and downtown Vancouver. Sit on the front porch on a summer's evening and you can see the dome of BC Place and watch the city light up behind it.

Growing up in that neighborhood had been like a kind of perpetual international summit. On our block alone, there were three Italian families, two Chinese, one Japanese, two German and another Scots family, like ours. Or not like ours. The McGoogans were the type of Scots people like to make fun of. "Hey, Jimmy!" you'd hear Iris call into the evening. "Stop that putterin' and gae in the house," though it would come out sounding a lot like *hoose*. "Supper's on the table and I dinna wanna miss me shows."

When they talked to my parents, they'd pine for the old country or they'd complain about the price of things. Once out of earshot, my father would say, "If they miss it so much, they should go back! Look at us—we've jobs and homes and good schools for the wee ones. Scotland's a nice place to visit, but Canada's my home."

And it was too. My mother and father and my older brother all applied for citizenship as soon as they were able. I was Canadian by birth. My parents and my brother were Canadian by choice. So we were all Canadians together, in our house on the Hill. But I grew up with the lilt of Scotland all around me.

"Nicole," my mother said as I let myself in the front door, "what a nice surprise." She's a petite redhead with flashing blue-green eyes, and today she was fully turned out. She didn't look like she should be in the kitchen at all.

84

"What's with the getup?" I asked.

"Some friends coming in for a bite," she said.

"Sorry, Mom. I should have called."

"Don't be silly, dear," she said, leading me back into the kitchen to continue her work while we chatted. "I always brag about you. You know that. It would be lovely to have you here in person so I can show you off."

I settled easily into old kitchen rhythms. I loaded things into the dishwasher, wiped the counters and generally made myself useful.

"Not a chance," I replied. "I'm outta here before anyone comes. Sorry. You remember what happened the last time?"

"That was nothing. It's just because you're so pretty."

Though she clearly remembered, I felt inclined to remind her. Just in case. "That Vivienne McPhee tried to set me up with her nephew. What's his name?"

"Hamish," my mom supplied.

"Yes, that's it. Hamish. As *if*."

"Now, now, dear. You don't know a thing about him."

"But I *do*. Ask Dad."

And now she laughed full out. "Oh, your dad! He's a fine one. Saying things like that. Hamish McPhee is..."

"A dork?"

She laughed. "No, Nicole. I was going to say he's a very nice young man. Let me see, what's he studying again...?"

"Podiatry. He's studying to be a foot doctor. Which, I assure you, is nothing like a brain surgeon, though you wouldn't know it to talk to him."

We laughed together.

"So, okay then. You're not here to meet up with Hamish. I understand. What *are* you doing here then? Mind, I love to see you, but we don't usually see you like this on a weekday. Is everything all right?"

Like I said, I'm lucky. And here's another one of the ways. My family is terrific. The older I get, the tighter my friendship with my mom seems to grow. My dad is strong and sweet and supportive. My brother and I travel in different circles, but he's human and decent and has grown to be a good man.

So I *could* have dumped all my troubles onto my mom. She would not only have listened, but helped me sort them out. But she was preparing a nice lunch, looking forward to an afternoon chatting with her girlfriends. And there would probably be lots of wine. For my mom, this was party time, and I didn't want to mess it up with my problems. And I *really, really* didn't want to bump into Vivienne McPhee.

"Sure, sure, Mom," I said. "Everything's just fine. I had to leave the office on a story and since I was in my car anyway…"

"You thought you'd look in on me and your dad. How nice! Sorry I don't have more time to spend, dear. Stir that pot. That's right, the one at the back. Stir it just a bit."

"Where's Dad?" I asked as I stirred. But I knew already.

Mom just looked at me, her eyebrows raised.

"Golf," I said.

My mom nodded.

"Where today?" I asked.

"Who knows? Oh, he tells me, but I don't always listen anymore. They're one like another to me, you know."

I laughed. I knew. My father had always been a bit of a golfer, but since he'd retired, he'd gone at it like a job. Most days he was out of the house by five or six o'clock in the morning, doing whatever golfing things required early-morning attention.

He'd generally be back by early to midafternoon and then he and mom would potter about together. They liked to shop. They liked to eat out. They liked to drive to the ocean and walk together. And they traveled a bit, but never without Dad's clubs.

"Right then," I said, giving the contents of the pot a final twirl. "I suppose I should get back to the office at some point."

My mom cleaned her hands, then crossed the kitchen to give me a hug. "Well, nice to see you, my girl. Are you sure you won't stay and have a wee chinwag with Viv?"

I stood back and looked down into her eyes and could see she was teasing me.

"Ummm...you know I'd love to, Mom..."

"Of course you would." There was a glint in her eye, laughter on her face. "You're just busy, is all. I'll tell her as much." Then I saw the laughter fade away. My mother looked suddenly serious and taller than her five foot one.

"Listen, my girl, I've a feeling you didn't come here today to talk about my hen party or your dad's golf." I started to protest, but she stopped me. "No, no, it's fine. I'm not going to press. I've just, as I said, a feeling. When you want, you come back and talk. Meanwhile, my darling, be careful."

TWELVE

I got back to my car, saw Itani's envelope sitting on the seat and had another thought.

"Mom, before I bounce," I said, back inside the house, "will you just take a quick look at this? See if you know what it is?"

"Sure, dear," she said. If she was curious, she kept it to herself. "I'll have a go."

I pulled the photo out of its envelope. She didn't hesitate. "Why, it's an ice pick," she said.

"An ice pick?" I repeated. "What's that? For mountaineering or something?"

"Oh no. Not at all. It's a kitchen tool. From long ago. They've not been in use in this country for a hundred years, I'd imagine. But I saw them at home when I was a lass."

"Used for…" I prompted.

"Chipping at ice, of course."

"Of course."

"No, truly. For making the block of ice fit in the coldbox, before there was such a thing as an electric fridge. Or for knocking a bit off for a drink and so on."

"You mean, like, in an icebox?"

"That's right."

"So it's a kitchen tool, you said?"

"I did."

Somehow, that made sense.

THIRTEEN

My maternal grandmother, long since departed, had what some call "the sight." I thought about that as I drove west along Broadway.

Granny Auden was, as my mom liked to say, "a wee bit funny." Which isn't to say she had a sense of humor. She did *not*. But she saw things in a different way.

When I was a kid, I used to wish that Granny's talent or gift would somehow rub off on me. But though I gave it serious thought and even a bit of practice, none of

Granny Auden's witchiness was ever mine. I was ordinary. Average even then.

My mother though. That was a different story. She was not wildly psychic. Mom's was a more gentle gift. She got feelings. Hunches. Like just now, when she'd looked into my eyes and told me to be careful. It wasn't like the warning another mother might give—a general warning against life's hidden dangers. Experience told me it was best to pay attention.

I found myself heading for the gallery. It was unlikely I'd find anything there, but I needed a starting point. And I couldn't think of a better place than at the beginning.

When he saw me, Sam's face lit up. "Why, if it isn't Nicole at Night! In the day, no less." He ushered me in. "What brings you to my humble place of business?"

The gallery looked different in the daylight. Smaller, somehow, without a crush of people filling it. Steve Marsh's show was still hung. As I looked around, I saw a lot of red dots.

"Everything is sold?" I said.

"It's sad, but yes, death will do that for an artist. The phone has been ringing off the hook all day. Suddenly everyone wants to get in." His hands fluttered helplessly. "And in this case, even more so, I think. It was so...*dramatic*, wasn't it? Him dying in the alley like that. It will be the talk of the town all month."

I made a mental note. As his dealer, Sam would have had something to gain from Marsh's death. Something financial. I looked the small man over carefully and decided that as far as suspects went, Sam wasn't much of one.

"But you haven't told me," he continued, "what brings you here today."

"I'm investigating the story," I said, trying to convince even myself. "The story of Steve Marsh's death."

"Oh." That hand again. "Oh, I see. I thought…that is to say…"

"You thought I only did the society pages."

"Well, I guess. But also, a reporter from your paper was here first thing this morning. He gave me the impression he was covering the story."

"We both kind of are." It wasn't *exactly* the truth, yet it was. I *was* covering the story. Brent just didn't know it yet. Nor did the city editor. But don't bother me with details. "We have…different perspectives."

I could see that Sam bought this. The inner workings of a newspaper are mysterious enough to most people that I didn't expect a lot of questions.

"In that case, I'll do everything I can to help. Of course. Steve Marsh was a very special client of mine. I just don't know what I can tell you that I didn't already tell Mr. Hartigan."

"That's okay. You can tell me the same stuff you told him. Sometimes, in the retelling, new details come to light. You said Steve was a special client. Let's start with that."

"Well, I discovered him." Sam thought for a second before continuing. "That's saying too much. He'd been painting for years before he tried to get representation. But when he showed me his work"—Sam put a hand to his collarbone, made that fluttering motion—"I just *swooned*." He led me over to the largest painting in the gallery. It was hung right in the center of the big space, on a wall suspended from the ceiling. Even last night, amid the crowd, I'd noticed both the piece and the pride of place.

The painting was huge. The background was bold, all angry reds and glaring greens. Slightly to the left of center was a young man, painted as though by a classical master. Dressed in torn jeans, a bandanna wrapped around his head. Unposed. He stood facing the artist boldly, as though he might spring from the canvas and punch anyone who got in his way. On one level, it was a portrait. But somehow, it was so much more. I said as much to Sam.

"Yes, yes," he said. "That's it exactly, isn't it? Another artist could make this painting and it would be ordinary. But"—Sam shook his head sadly—"Steve saw the beauty in this. He saw it and incorporated everything one could see. And perhaps everything that couldn't be seen."

This confused me. "How can you paint what you can't see?"

"That's the very essence of art, I think," he said. "Anyone can paint what anyone can see. But to paint in a way that makes you *feel* something? That's mastery."

I looked at the title of the painting. "*Eldert*?"

"Yes, yes," he said again. "Isn't it wonderful? Just *Eldert*. So in a sense, it is just a painting of this young man. And yet..."

"Who is he?" I asked. "Who is Eldert?"

Sam looked at me, surprised. "You don't know much about this artist then?"

I shook my head.

He went over to a rack at the side of the gallery and pulled out a brochure. I wasn't surprised to see that *Eldert* had been chosen to adorn the cover. It was a powerful work. "Here, you can read this. It'll explain Steve's work and, in a sense, the man."

"Thanks. Can I take this?"

Sam nodded.

I tucked it into my bag. "Did you know Steve's girlfriend? Caitlen Benton-Harris?"

"Yes, of course. I've met her on many occasions." It was possibly my imagination, but I thought I saw a moue of distaste.

"Did you see her here last night?" I asked.

Sam pondered for a moment. "Now that you mention it," he said finally, "I didn't. Hmmmm...that's odd."

By the time Caitlen had arrived, Steve was dead and Sam was occupied elsewhere.

"Do you know where I can find her?"

"I'm sorry, but I don't. She'd show up with Steve sometimes. I don't have a number for her. I had no reason to call her."

"Of course. What does she do?" I asked. "Where does she work?"

"She's an artist too. She once asked me to represent her."

"And you wouldn't?"

"No. Not then. The work was too raw," he explained, "too unfinished. I told her to come back when she had some more miles on her. Honestly, though? I was being kind. I didn't see anything that made me think she had what it takes."

"And what does it take?" I asked.

"Well, a lot of things, really. But one thing is key. Talent."

"You're saying she lacked talent?"

"It sounds harsh, I suppose. But yes. I guess that's it all right."

"And Steve had that?"

"Talent? Oh yes! Steve did. And so much more. You never met him?"

I shook my head, trying not to think of the dead man in his car. That didn't count.

"Steve was...well, he was extraordinary. I don't know how else to say it."

There was something in Sam's face. Or a shadow of something.

"You guys were close?"

"Oh no. Not really." Sam shrugged. "I was his dealer. That is a special relationship in its own right."

"You said his paintings are selling well now. Better than when he was alive?"

"As I said, that can be what happens when an artist dies. And when that happens? Well, people line up for opportunity, don't they?"

FOURTEEN

On my way back to the office, I thought about what I knew so far. While the ice-pick thing was huge, I'd promised Itani I wouldn't use it for three days. That meant that in three days I'd have an exclusive on the ice pick. This was a byline there was no way Brent was going to wrangle from me. But I didn't think one story would be enough. I needed to make such a splash and impact that I'd secure a position in the newsroom once a spot opened.

Brent was already on the elevator when I got in at the parking level.

"Well, well," he said with a little smirk, "here's our talented gossip columnist. And tell me, please, what will Nicole be up to on this night?"

No word on my absent byline, my stolen opening paragraph. Nothing at all, really, beyond the patronizing emptiness I'd always gotten from him.

I groped for an answer that would stop him in his tracks, shut him up and remove the smirk from his face as though by a kick from my pointy-toed shoe to his groin. I couldn't think of anything.

When the elevator doors opened for him, I gave up. I felt the defeat through my whole body. He got off the elevator and I'd barely looked at him. As the doors closed, I heard him call out sweetly, "Have a nice day, Nicole."

I stood for a moment in the empty elevator, my heart pounding. He'd put me in my place without ever lifting his voice.

We'd had some kind of contest. He had won.

"Prick," I said, just as I had the night before. I retreated to my cubicle with a fearsome relief. This was home, I told myself. This was safe. As I sat at my desk, I fingered the neat stacks of invitations. I looked at the corkboard where I'd pinned up a couple of choice photos and some nice memories. "Nicole at Night" was mine. No one would contest me for it, no one would take it away. I was good at it, I told myself. And the parties were fun. There were aspects of the job that I really loved.

The food was great. Event food all the time. Canapés and caviar and cheese and tiny wontons served on delicate spoons... my grocery bill was next to nothing, just eggs and bread and Earl Grey tea.

The notoriety. That was fun. It was like I was famous, though in a small enough dose that it wasn't irritating. My drycleaner gave me special treatment, rushed my stuff right through. At the market, the occasional checkout girl would recognize me from my picture in the paper and be gently flustered and admiring. The best part of fame. Not so much that you needed to watch your steps or that people asked for your autograph over dinner. Just enough that people were nice to you when they realized who you were. That was pleasant. I'd gotten used to a world that was nice to me.

All those things were good, and I was safe. Why would anyone want anything else? As I thought these things, I realized something. Brent was a master manipulator. The impossible-to-get quote. The illusive interview. The access behind closed doors. Not all reporters have this gift, but some do. It explained how he could he make me feel so small with a word and a glance. I pulled myself up and felt as though I was adding steel to my spine. I felt mad and determined and yet serene. I knew what I wanted. And I knew how to get it.

I pushed aside my self-doubt and reached for the phone.

FIFTEEN

"Good afternoon, Giggling Gourmet," a chipper voice said on the other end of the line. "This is Terese. Can I help you?"

"Hey, Terese, this is Nicole Charles from the *Vancouver Post*. I was wondering if I could ask you a few questions?"

"Hi, Nicole!" It was a gush. Caterers are among those who always recognize me. They're probably big readers, scouring my column daily looking for mentions of them or their food. "I would *love* to talk to you, but it's mad here today.

We're getting ready for an event in under an hour and there's a lot to do. Can it hold until tomorrow—no, scratch that." She didn't even let me answer. "We've got a lunch and two evening events. The best thing might be for you to drop by in person. We're always busy, but we can blab while we work." She rattled off an address near Granville Island, then hung up before I could respond.

I did a final check of my email, adjusted my schedule and headed out the door.

Giggling Gourmet operated out of a brightly painted reclaimed brick building near the public market. I pushed the bright orange door open on a lime-green reception area with a purple ceiling. A rug in front of the empty reception desk was the color of milk chocolate. A lamp was a vibrant lilac that cast a purplish glow over the yellow walls. But not the ceiling, of course, since that was purple already.

Industry awards were hung on the wall, so despite the goofy name, Giggling Gourmet knew what it was about. If I stood very still and listened very hard, I could hear it. Giggling. If that wasn't enough of an invitation, the wonderful food smells were. I followed the sounds and smells to the kitchen.

As goofy as the reception area and the name were, the kitchen was all business. Surgically clean stainless steel from bottom to top. Half a dozen young women were involved in various stages of food prep. And, of course, giggling. The giggling died when they noticed me standing there. And then: "Nicole!" It was a chorus from three of the six voices. I guess I'll never get any closer to feeling like a pop star.

Wiping hands on aprons, they mobbed me. And I guess in their world, I *was* a celebrity. I was someone who had the power to make a good business better. If only

I would slide a word in here, a photo there. You couldn't buy the kind of advertising I could dole out with a single nod. That's a big responsibility. I don't take it lightly.

I saw a tall blond with long legs and a delicate pot belly under a smeared apron wipe her hands harder than the others, then extend one of them to me.

"Hi, Nicole," she said, smiling. "I'm Terese. We spoke on the phone." And then, "Back to it, ladies. The food for the Zimmerman batmitzvah isn't going to walk there on its own."

At her words, the little crowd dispersed throughout the kitchen, but none of them were out of earshot. Terese led me over to the station where she'd been working. A vat of tasty-looking chicken in a cream sauce stood next to pastry casings.

"I *really* have to finish this vol-au-vent," she explained. "But we can talk. We talk all the time."

"We do," chimed in the girl working nearest us, a half dozen piercings in her left ear. "We talk nonstop!" She was chopping madly—carrots, onions, celery—and dropping bits into a huge pot while she talked.

"On the phone, you said you had questions," Terese said, expertly stuffing the pastry shells.

"I'm covering the death of Steve Marsh," I explained. I was the gossip columnist. I understood the question in her look. I decided not to reply to it.

"I spoke with someone from the paper this morning. Buzz somebody."

"Brent?" I asked. "Brent Hartigan?"

"I think so," she said. "I didn't have much time for him. We were getting ready for a lunch thing."

"On the phone," I said. It wasn't a question. She *would* have made time if she'd seen him. Probably wouldn't have forgotten his name either. Brent is *that* hot.

"Right," she said, still stuffing. "I'm sorry, but there wasn't anything to tell him. I was there the whole time—"

"So was I," a voice chimed in behind me.

"Me too," said another from across the room.

"—but I didn't see anything."

"We couldn't, could we?" said someone across the room. I looked over at a faunlike girl who didn't look big enough to manage the Dutch oven she was moving across the room. "A lot of people. A big-deal event."

Terese nodded agreement. "Big, big deal. We've done bigger parties, of course. But they pulled all the stops."

"Why?" I asked.

Terese shrugged over her work. "I don't know. I don't ask those kind of questions. Just make the food."

"And cash the checks," said earrings girl, madly chopping.

"I think it was his grandfather." This was the faunlike girl, now finished moving her Dutch oven and carefully stirring her brew on the stove.

"His grandfather?" I said.

"Well, isn't he rich and famous?"

I nodded. Shrugged. I hadn't thought about the fact that Marsh's family might have been paying for some of his gallery activities. But it was worth thinking about.

Terese nodded. "You know, I think Ann might be right. I mean, we've been super busy, and I hadn't really stopped to think of anything but work."

"And work and work and work," a voice grumbled from across the room. Terese shot her a glance and a grin and went on.

"Yeah. *And* work. But when I think of it, it was way over the top for a gallery opening. You know, they ordered ten pounds of *beluga* for last night. For blini and caviar."

I blinked. I did enough of my major eating at events to know that ten pounds was a *lot* of beluga. And blini and caviar just did not show up at gallery openings.

"And the oyster bar," knife-and-earrings added. "Don't forget the oyster bar."

Terese rolled her eyes. "One will not forget that, will one?" she said in clipped tones.

I wanted to ask—I really did—and Terese so obviously wanted to tell me, but we were getting offtrack.

"So...okay. You were super busy at the event. Did you notice any weird comings and goings out of the back door?"

Terese lifted her eyes from her work to shoot me a disbelieving glance. "Seriously? At a *gallery* opening? There was nothing *but* weird comings and goings."

"Still," I insisted, "the guest of honor ended up dead. Anything you might remember could be helpful."

"Now you're a cop?" It was knife-and-earrings, though by now she'd put the knife down and was shredding ginger with a tool that looked like it belonged in a woodworking shop.

"I'm not a cop," I said solidly. "But investigative journalists have been known to be extremely helpful in uncovering and exposing criminal behavior and activities." I don't know where the words came from. Some manual from Journalism 101, I expect. But I flushed as I said them and wished I could take them back.

"What book did you get *that* out of?" said the girl with the earrings, whom I was starting to think about not liking.

"Ingrid, c'mon. Play nice." This was Terese.

Ingrid shrugged and went back to her ginger.

"Well, we didn't see anything. We talked about it after, of course. We haven't talked about much else all day. And we'd hired on extra serving staff for the event. None of them saw anything either."

"You talked about it?"

Terese nodded. "We went for a drink afterward. We were so shaken. And we all agreed. We saw a lot of people coming and going. A lot. People were going out there to smoke. Some people were parked back there. But there was no one that caught the attention of any of the catering staff."

I felt something inside me that had been hopeful crumble slightly. Terese sounded sure. They'd discussed it among themselves and come up with zip. I wasn't surprised. It was too much to ask to find a solid lead this early in—I knew *that* from journalism school as well. Still. It would have been amazing to uncover something significant at this stage. Something Brent hadn't gotten.

"What about Buddy?" Sioban asked suddenly.

I felt my ears prick up.

"Buddy?" I asked.

Terese wiped her hands furiously again, walked over to a small desk in the corner of the room, flipped through an old-fashioned Rolodex and extracted a business card.

"Buddy Gareth. You might want to talk to him. We use him on a lot of our jobs," Terese said, handing me the card. I turned it over, saw a dove's wing that looked like glass. Turned it back again. *Buddy Gareth*, it said in plain black lettering. And under it, larger: *The Ice Man.*

SIXTEEN

On my way to the Pan Pacific Hotel, I tried Buddy's number and got voice mail.

Rock music. Something thick and old. And over the music, "Hey, you've reached the Ice Man. Leave your digits and I'll slide ya back."

I left my digits, then promptly forgot about him as I parked my car at the Pan Pacific. I didn't realize I'd forgotten the name of the event I was attending until I stood in the hotel foyer and checked the board.

It came back to me when the words *Art for Schizophrenia* caught my eye. Now, art by itself is not funny, and certainly schizophrenia is no laughing matter, but the two of them together? To me it felt like mushroom gravy on ice cream. I couldn't reconcile them as a set.

I braced myself for the sight of painting schizophrenics and was disappointed when I pulled open the ballroom door and saw a crowd that looked like every other fundraising group I'd ever encountered.

I checked the room quickly, trying to determine if any of my bosses were there, then made a beeline for the buffet table, slowing only to take a glass of wine from a passing tray.

Either I was very hungry or the food was super good, because before I'd even introduced myself to anyone or taken any pictures, I found a standing-height table in a far corner and began to stuff my face.

"I wish I could do that." The voice was masculine. And nearby.

He was standing at the next table with a cocktail glass in hand, dressed in a tuxedo that was obviously not a rental and looking as at home in it as other men do in chinos. There was something familiar about him, but I couldn't put my finger on it.

I swallowed the canapé I'd been working on and said, "Why can't you?"

He moved to my table.

"I'm on the organizing committee for this event, for one. That puts me in a sort of host position. And it wouldn't do for the host to be seen loading up on the grub."

"It wouldn't?" I said. "Why not?"

"I'm meant to be mingling and taking people's money from their wallets."

"But you're not doing that now."

"Maybe I am," he said smugly. "Maybe that's why I chose this moment to come speak to you. You were vulnerable with all that food in hand."

I shook my head. "I don't think so."

"Why not?"

I indicated my jacket. "Not enough brass buttons." Then my hair. "And my highlights plainly didn't cost enough."

"All right. You have me there. So why am I here talking to you?" It was in his eyes, the reason. And in his voice, startlingly intimate even while he spoke of things that were not.

"It's my food," I said. "You thought, Look at that girl. She's small. I can push her over easily and grab something off her plate."

"Is that what I thought?"

"You did. But here." I snagged a piece of white asparagus from my plate and handed it to him. "I'll save you the trouble. It wouldn't look good, you pushing me to the floor. What with you playing host and all."

He took the asparagus, bit the top off gingerly, then reached across and put it gently back on the edge of my plate. "Thank you," he said seriously. "You've saved me from falling down in a hungry heap."

"You're welcome," I said. "Now what will you do?"

"I've got hosting duties, don't I? And checks to seduce from willing hands. You're not leaving right away, are you?"

"No. I'm not," I agreed.

As he walked away, I found that I liked watching him move.

He started chatting with a beautiful brunette in a clingy dress. He responded to something she said with a laugh that was more than polite. Just then, he lifted his head and looked straight into my eyes. I flushed at the look and hoped he hadn't noticed in the room's dim light.

I pulled myself together and got to work. He'd finished chatting with the clingy brunette, so I crossed to her and chatted her up myself, knowing her cleavage would be the perfect fit for my column.

Before long we were joined by a tall blond in a jade-green dress. More cleavage. When a third friend showed up—a redhead this time—I knew I had my money shot. I lined them up near the sign about arts and schizophrenia.

As I got ready to leave, I looked around but didn't see the beautiful man in the custom tux. It was unsurprising to me that Prince Charming would show up early and be gone before the evening became full. Story of my life.

And then he was there, standing right in front of me.

"Trying to get away?" he said.

I smiled back, asking my heart to be still.

"Not trying. This isn't my only party tonight. I have to run, but it was nice to have met you," I said, extending my hand. "I'm Nicole Charles."

He smiled at that. "I know who you are, Nicole," he said, taking my hand. "I'm Reston Marsh."

SEVENTEEN

It was hard, after that, to keep my mind on my job. I tried to connect the dots. Had I ever heard Reston Marsh's name before? It didn't ring any bells. How many society Marsh families could there be in Vancouver?

And Reston Marsh had sought me out, I knew he had. Why? Sure, I was an attractive young woman alone at a charity function. But the place was crawling with attractive women.

"Are you related to the artist Steve Marsh?" I asked.

"Yeah. Our fathers are brothers."

"So he was your cousin?"

"That's right."

"Not close, I guess?"

"No," he said. "We weren't. You might say we lived on different sides of the tracks."

"On which side of the tracks did he live?"

"All that artsy stuff. He had an apartment in Yaletown and a studio at 1000 Parker."

I didn't think Yaletown was the wrong side of the tracks. It also wasn't a surprise. I'd known where he lived. But the studio? That was news to me.

"You guys weren't close," I said again.

"What makes you keep saying that?"

"You're here instead of off crying in your beer someplace. I did the math."

"Well, we weren't tight, but we weren't unfriendly. Some bad blood with our dads when they were kids, so Steve-o and I never really hung out."

"Bad blood?"

"Something about his dad, I think it was. But no one was ever really talking about it."

"What about his girlfriend?"

"Caitlen?"

"Sure," I said.

"We've both known her since school. I never got it, really. She always seemed a cold one to me."

"In what way?"

He looked at me carefully. "Off the record?"

"Okay."

"She was never quite right."

"Right?"

"Just this"—he searched for the right word—"distance? She just wasn't someone you could talk to. Even when we were kids."

"Did they live together?"

To my surprise, he laughed. "Oh no. Steve lived in Yaletown."

"I know."

"But I'm pretty sure Caitlen had a place on English Bay."

"That seems an odd detail for you to know."

"Not really. Our family has owned the building for decades. I got the idea Caitlen's family had money problems a few years ago. Steve had to get the family trust to approve her living there. This is turning into quite the little interrogation."

I indicated the party still going on around us. "Just doing my job. But now that you mention it, you did seem awful eager to talk to me. What was that about?"

He reached out then. Slid one smooth hand down my bare arm. Looked straight into my eyes.

"You have to ask?"

We didn't talk anymore about work or dead cousins after that.

EIGHTEEN

There was flirting. Digits exchanged. Arrangements made for an unspecified dinner at some future point. I took some photos and left.

There were three more stops. By the time I was done and got to 1000 Parker, it was 11:30. I told myself I was just driving by on my way home. It was too late to be bugging people. But there were lights on all over the place, and I figured if I peeked right then, it would save me a few steps in the morning. The thought of Hartigan closing in was never far from my mind.

In Vancouver art circles, 1000 Parker is well known. A huge old beast of a building in a crappy part of town. Outside it looks like a warehouse. Inside it's worse. Until you get behind the doors in the maze, to where the magic is made.

I'd been to events at 1000 Parker. Every fall the Eastside Culture Crawl brought thousands of people through the building. But most of the time, it was just as it was tonight. Lots of studios where artists worked behind battered doors and windowed entries.

I looked for a directory but didn't see one. When a bearded man with multiple piercings came out of a studio and looked at me curiously, I returned the look, then asked if he knew where I could find Steve Marsh's studio.

"The dead guy, right?"

I nodded.

"I think he was up on the third floor." He directed me up a couple of stairways, across an elevated walkway and up another stairway to the top floor.

As I made my way through the building, I heard more signs of life than I saw. Bare wood floors, blank gray doors. I tried not to think about rats when I heard scuttling in corners.

When I reached my destination the studio was dark and the lights off. The lock looked serious. Not high security, but beyond my nonexistent B-and-E skills. There was a pane of glass on either side of the door. It wasn't flimsy. But neither was it security grade.

It was late. There was no one in sight. And it didn't seem like the kind of place that would have an alarm. That, and the very real possibility I'd find something Brent didn't have, spurred me one. Before I could stop myself, I took off my shoe, pointed the heel at the glass closest to the doorknob and gave the pane a resounding *thwack*. It didn't shatter right away. It took a second tap. And then a third. But when it shattered, it did so completely. I didn't have to push any glass out of my way before I reached around and opened the door from the inside.

I found the lights and looked around. A desk and computer were pushed against one wall with a couple of filing cabinets. Stacks of painted canvases leaned against both side walls, and at the end of the room, in a window I imagined would be filled with light during the day, sat two large easels.

One of the easels held a painting. The work in progress was different than what I'd already seen of Marsh's work. The subject matter was starkly different. A man on a boat. A different era, but something familiar in his face. The boat was long and low and wood. *Fleetwood* in script text on her stern. It looked like it was on a river. I didn't know what I was looking at. I was sure of that. But I knew it was something to see.

I looked around some more. Nothing unexpected on the desk. The computer was password protected. The bookcases held books. The filing cabinets, files. I kept poking, losing hope as I did so until I came across a letter. It was neatly folded in an addressed envelope that had clearly not been sent. Dated three days earlier, it was from Steve to Sam at the gallery. In formal language, it terminated their agreement, effective the first of the upcoming month. I rested my butt on the edge of the desk while I thought back over my interactions with Sam. I was certain there had been no hint that there was anything wrong between Sam and the artist he said he'd discovered.

Steve had intended to end the relationship. And now Steve was dead.

NINETEEN

By the time I got back to my place, I was so tired it was all I could do to keep from just dropping into bed fully dressed. The extra effort I was putting into covering a crime had pushed me over the top of my resources. Still, I had work to do. I uploaded the evening's photos to my computer. I went through and organized them, wrote a few captions and some inane copy, then filed my column to the *Post*'s news server for the early edition.

I was just about to drop into bed when I saw something sticking out of my bag.

The brochure Sam had given me at the gallery. I'd forgotten about it. I read more about Steve's background with interest. I wasn't surprised to discover that there really was someone in Steve's life named Eldert. It was there in the brochure, in the extract below the picture of the painting.

Eldert Harris was the son of my grandfather's best friend. The friendship ended badly and Eldert took on his father's legacy of anger. The painting before you was created from my imagination. That's how I think of Eldert: angry and passionate for a reason. So much that happens between us as humans doesn't get washed away by the water of life.

The water of life. I was suddenly wide awake. I grabbed my laptop and went back to Google. The first entries I found meant nothing to me. The phrase was often tied into Christian ideology. I hadn't known that, but it wasn't what I was after. I read a bunch of definitions until I saw that the phrase could refer to "a concentrated solution of ethanol." More online searches.

"Booze," I said.

So much that happens between us as humans doesn't get washed away by the water of life.

There was something I was missing, that was clear. But what?

TWENTY

I was so tired I would have slept all day had my phone not started ringing in the morning. I checked the time as I pulled it toward me. Eight fifteen. And I didn't recognize the number.

"This is Buddy Gareth," a man's voice said when I answered.

"The Ice Man," I said before I thought about it.

He sounded pleased. "Yes. That's right."

I asked him much the same as I had of the caterers the day before. The big difference was that he knew something.

"I saw Steve getting into his car just after I installed the ice sculpture."

"Before the opening?"

"That's right. Maybe half an hour. And I thought it was odd."

"What was?"

"Well, it was his big night, wasn't it? You wouldn't think he'd leave."

"And you're sure it was him?"

"Absolutely. I didn't really know who he was before I was contacted for a sculpture. Then I paid attention, you know? Celebrity client."

"But you thought it odd he was leaving? Had he just forgotten something? Or was going to pick someone up? Or—"

"No, sure," he interrupted. "I thought about all that stuff. But I saw them arguing. Then he just took off, you know? Like someone was chasing him."

"Arguing?"

"I mentioned that, I think."

"You did not. Tell me now."

The Ice Man described an argument in the gallery between Steve and a man. What man? The Ice Man didn't know.

"He was blond and kinda girly, you know?"

I told him I did. "What was said?"

Buddy couldn't tell me. He'd been too far away to hear.

"But then he left, just as I was leaving. That's when he almost slammed into the old man."

"Old man?"

"I mentioned that."

"You did not."

"Pretty sure the old guy was waiting for him. They had words, like, fast, you know?"

While the two argued, the ice man had gone on his own way.

"Let me get this straight." After finding out a whole lot of nothing, hearing all of *this* was a gift. I wanted to make sure I got it right. "You saw Marsh arguing in the gallery with an effeminate, blond man. Then you saw him outside, arguing with another, older man. But you don't know how it ended."

"But I do. Steve Marsh ended up dead."

After I got off the phone, I went over the small pieces I'd uncovered. There was Eldert Harris and his water of life. There were Steve's arguments with a couple of men, along with the agency termination agreement I'd found at the studio. The fact that the show had sold out once Steve was dead was never far from my mind. And Caitlen's lateness at the opening still struck me as curious.

It was a gorgeous day and I felt like stretching my legs, so I headed toward Granville Island on foot. I grabbed a coffee at the Blue Parrot in the market, then wandered up along the shore, past Bridges Restaurant and the party boats moored nearby and up along the walkway at the seashore that got so much less traffic than the main entranceway to the island.

This walk, coffee in hand, has always been a peaceful respite for me. A place to think and reflect. So when I looked up and saw a familiar hull tied up in one of the marinas, I almost discounted what my eyes told me was truth.

I was so anxious to get to the boat I'd seen, I had to stop myself from running along the wharf. I told myself I couldn't be right. But how could I possibly be wrong?

When I got to her I tried to keep down my excitement. She was old and wooden and absolutely right. I couldn't imagine that this was not the boat from the painting. She was moored on a finger, bow in, so I couldn't see the name to confirm. But when I got closer, a man's voice distracted me just as I read the name *Fleetwood* stenciled on the stern.

"You lost, young lady?"

The man who peered at me from the boat's interior was beyond elderly. He was old.

"I'm...I'm not," I stammered.

"Explain yourself then." Despite his extreme age, as he came out of the cabin he looked fit and upright. His voice was tinged with dust, but it held steel.

"This boat. I saw it. In a painting." It was all I could do to keep from stammering.

"And you are...?" he asked, making me think he wasn't a regular reader of my paper.

"I'm Nicole Charles, sir. I'm a reporter with the *Vancouver Post*."

"And what might a newspaper be wanting with me?"

"It's not the paper, sir. It's this boat. As I said. I saw it. In a painting."

"Not one like it?"

"No, sir. It was called *Fleetwood*."

"That does seem a strange coincidence."

"Yes, sir."

"Well, what can I do for you?"

"Nothing, Mr...." It was then I realized he hadn't given me his name.

"Harris," he said, extending one leathery mitt. "Eldert Harris."

"How do you do, sir." Inside I was hesitating. And it didn't take me long to formulate the question. "Are you related to Caitlen Benton-Harris?"

"My granddaughter."

"Do you know her boyfriend, Steve Marsh?"

His face darkened. "I did. Marsh. He's dead."

"Sir, forgive me, but I have to ask. I was told that Marsh had words with someone who meets your description not long before he died."

"Did you now?" To my discomfort, the old man looked amused.

"Yes, sir. I did."

"Did this 'someone' also tell you that Marsh had been cheating on my granddaughter?"

"No, sir. I haven't heard even a whisper of that."

"Well, it's true. He told me, that day, that he'd broken it off. That he was going to finally ask Caitlen to marry him because he was free. I told him I didn't care. They're a bad lot, those Marshes."

"Are you saying you didn't kill him?"

"Me? Honestly? I wouldn't dirty my hands. Anyway, better or worse? Caitlen loved him. And I think, after a fashion, he loved her as well."

"She didn't kill him?"

"Caitlen? Don't be daft. She had more to lose than gain if she got rid of him."

"Can I ask who he was having an affair with?"

"I'm not going to tell you that, no. Ask Caitlen herself. If she wants you to know, she'll say."

As I walked back home, my mind was racing. Once in the door, I grabbed my laptop. Reporters have access to good online tools, but I didn't need any of those today. Fifteen minutes with Google filled in some of the blanks, though I needed to bring out a steno pad and take notes in order to keep track.

Eldert Harris was the son of the original rum-running Harris, Ebenezer. Ebenezer had been partners with Phineas Marsh, but where Phineas Marsh and his descendants ended up with a fortune, Ebenezer Harris ended up dying in jail in Walla Walla, Washington, near the end of 1930.

The things that had bound Steve Marsh and Caitlen Harris were deep and old, and, it seemed, both had been aware of this. The connection of these two might even have righted an ancient wrong. I drew myself up, chided myself. I was just being dramatic. Romantic. But a picture was beginning to emerge. I knew who I had to talk to next.

TWENTY-ONE

A quick call to Itani had supplied me with an address. She'd gotten it from Steve Marsh's cell phone.

The Rosewood Building on Beach Avenue was built in 1928. Itani didn't tell me that, a plaque on the building did. The building wasn't tall, but it was beautiful. Just five stories of nothing but charm. A place built for rich people who wanted to pretend they were living some-place warm. There was a buzzer, but I didn't want to use it. I waited at a discreet distance until a slow-moving matron came into the foyer with three tiny dogs. I darted forward to give her a hand with the door.

"Thank you, my dear!" she exclaimed as she went out.

"Don't mention it," I said from inside.

"So many young people are not polite these days," she said as she and the dogs made their way down Beach.

If there's one thing I am, it's polite.

Itani had told me Caitlen was in 106, which I found without much trouble. When she opened the door, I could tell I was the last person she expected or wanted to see. She started to close the door so quickly, I was glad I'd thought to stick my foot in it just as it opened.

"You," she said in a voice that said she remembered me.

"May I ask you a few questions?"

"You may not. In fact, if you get your foot out of my door, I'll close it."

"Eldert Harris," I said. It wasn't a question, but it got her attention anyway.

"Is he okay?" The concern on her face was real.

"He's fine. I was just wondering about your connection to him."

"Excuse me?"

I planted my foot more firmly in the door.

"He's your grandfather?"

"Yes, that's right."

"But he was also your boyfriend's enemy."

"Please. Get your foot out of my door." She squeezed the door on it so tightly, I could feel tears starting. I held on and hoped like hell my foot wasn't broken.

"Your grandfather is the enemy of your boyfriend," I insisted.

"But that's ridiculous," she said, though she didn't ease the pressure on my foot.

"I don't think so."

"Steve didn't have any enemies." Her gaze was innocent. And blue.

"There's an ice pick at the cop shop says that's not true," I said, though I felt bad when I saw her pale at my words.

"Please. Why are you doing this? Just leave me be."

"Your grandfather killed Steve Marsh!" There. I'd said it aloud.

"No." She shook her head, firm and confident. And I bought it. Whatever *was* true, this woman didn't know about it. I sailed on anyway.

"Sure. He's hated the whole Marsh family since he was in jail and Phineas Marsh stayed free and—"

She interrupted me. It didn't take a genius to know she was glad to be able to do so.

"That's ridiculous. My grandfather was never in jail. He was really only a boy himself when his father—Eldert Senior—died in jail."

"Senior?"

"That's right." She stopped fighting with the door now and stood back on her heels, her arms crossed in front of her, looking pleased.

"I've made a mistake," I said. And now that she'd said it, and I did the math, it was the only obvious thing. The man I'd met had been very young when the bad blood between the Marshes and the Harrises had been spun. "I'm sorry."

"You're sorry? Imagine how sorry I am. Steve not two days gone and you here accusing my poor grandfather of God knows what."

"But it all made so much sense." I could feel my sketchy theories crumbling in the face of her confidence.

"My grandfather *was* upset with Steve," Caitlen said. Her voice was slightly softer now. I had the feeling she might even be feeling a little sorry for me. "But not for the reasons you think." She shifted her eyes left and right, as though searching for the answer to a question that hadn't been asked.

Then she surprised me by saying, "Why don't you just come in?" I was too startled to do anything but follow her inside.

The living room had a wonderful view of the beach at English Bay, but I barely noticed. Caitlen directed me to sit on a long white sofa, perching herself opposite me on a matching chair.

"The thing is, Gramps found out that Steve was having an affair."

"So he went to talk to him? Isn't that a little—?"

"Extreme?" Caitlen supplied. "Absolutely. But he's very protective of me."

"You see how this looks."

"I do. But I'm sure Gramps didn't kill him."

"How can you be certain?"

"Because I think I know who did."

Caitlen told me a story. It was one that made sense and also confirmed what her grandfather had told me at the *Fleetwood*.

I sat with her for the better part of an hour, occasionally interjecting with a question but mostly listening to a tale that was obviously difficult for her to tell. Sometimes while she talked, she cried.

"But why didn't you tell the police?"

She looked at me. "I thought about it. Truly I did. But answer me this—would you have?"

Afterward, I got back in my car and headed in the direction of the Cambie Street Bridge. I could have told Itani with a phone call, but I wanted to be with her when she rolled out to make the arrest. That would even be in my story—the cops rolling out. I was going to get my byline. There was no way Hartigan could have scooped me on any of this. Turns out that's another thing they don't teach you in journalism school: every truly good ending has a big twist.

TWENTY-TWO

After I met with Itani, I wrote the story as quickly as I could. I was scared Hartigan might get wind of even part of it and break it ahead of me. But he did not. There were details I left out. I knew I'd clean up some of those in follow-up stories over the next few weeks.

When I was done, I didn't even upload my piece to the server. I put it on a thumb drive and walked it down to the fourth floor, where I put it into Mike's hands.

"I don't want Hartigan's mitts on this," I said. I sat on the chair opposite his desk, trying not to try to read his face while he read.

"Good work, Nic," he said when he was done. "Far as I know, the art dealer wasn't even a suspect."

"That's right."

"And Steve had been having an affair with him? Your source is good?"

"The best. His fiancé, Caitlen Benton-Harris."

Mike whistled.

"Exactly," I said. "Steve was using him, Mike. He tried to end it some time ago, but the dealer was in love with him. Plus Steve still needed him to sell his work. But recently he started getting bigger. Caitlen told me Steve had an offer from a gallery in Toronto that would have taken his work international."

"So Steve was going to end it."

"Right. Which would have meant the end of these growing commissions, not to mention the relationship. So Sam kills Marsh outside the gallery, which is perfect. Not only does it secure Sam's position as agent of a fairly large body of work, but the timing and location—right outside the gallery where Steve's show was opening— meant that the publicity from the killing alone would make Sam a fortune."

"You said the show sold out by the next day."

"It did. Plus there were stacks and stacks of finished canvases at the studio and more in the basement at the gallery when they went to arrest Sam. Steve was prolific."

Mike whistled. "So hundreds of thousands?"

"In commissions, yes. I did a rough calculation. The gross from sales of everything we know about would have been in the millions."

"But the ice pick, Nic. Why the hell use an ice pick?"

"Itani says that's the best news of this whole thing. Without it, Sam might have gotten away with manslaughter. But the ice pick indicates premeditation. See, Sam was trying to frame Caitlen's grandfather."

"You've indicated that in the story. I'm still not sure I get why."

"He was in the rum-running business with Marsh's great-grandfather when he was a kid. His own father went to prison. Sam knew all of that and thought he could make it look like Old Man Harris did the deed for revenge of crimes against his family."

"And the ice pick?" Mike prompted again.

"It wasn't from Harris's boat. The police think there might be no actual connection with Harris, but it's definitely from that era."

"So it *could* have been from that boat, which was all that mattered."

"Exactly."

I asked if I'd be moving downstairs.

Mike shook his head. "You did a good job, kid. But we're set down here just now. And I gather things are not so set upstairs."

I couldn't help myself. I sighed. "Gossip."

"That's right." He gave me a crooked grin. "It's a tough job, kid. But someone's gotta do it. You can be proud of yourself on this one though. You did a good job reporting. And you uncovered some stuff I'm pretty sure no one else would have done. You can give yourself a pat on the back."

I just looked at him.

"Okay. That's not what you want to hear. I get it. But it's all I've got right now. Maybe things could have been different, but you and Hartigan don't play well together—"

"It's not my fault!" I interrupted.

"I have no doubt of that at all. I've met him, right? It's just so much more compli- cated than all of that. Budgets and head counts and so on. Plus they need someone on your beat, right?"

Budgets and head counts and being good at something that wasn't my dream. Still, there were worse fates. Much worse.

I'd turned to head back up to the fifth floor when Brent's voice stopped me.

"Good job, Nic," he said as he came in.

"Thanks." And I meant it. But at the same time, I was waiting for the other shoe.

"You never told me how you knew."

"Pardon?"

"You were so cool about everything. How did you put it together? No one else had a clue."

"I didn't."

Now it was his turn to be confused.

"Not really. I mean, I had some hunches. And I asked some questions. Got the right answers."

Hartigan nodded, grunted something and went on his way. But his question left me thinking. That was really all reporting ever was. At its finest, it was asking the right questions, getting the hoped-for answers. I was good at it. I hadn't achieved my goal of being a reporter—a real reporter. Yet. But I would. I knew that too.

AUTHOR'S NOTE

There is a special kind of natural beauty to the syntax of noir. In writing and then editing *If It Bleeds*, I felt that language pushed beyond the places it normally goes. It felt like a dance and was certainly a challenge, and I'm grateful to Bob Tyrrell, Ruth Linka and the whole team at Orca Books for the important commitment they've made to the Rapid Read series. I'm very proud that they asked me to dance.

Thanks to David Middleton and Michael Karl Richards for their continued support and artistic guidance.

LINDA L. RICHARDS is a journalist and award-winning author. She is the founding editor of *January Magazine*, one of the Web's most respected voices about books. She is also the author of six novels and several works of nonfiction and is on the faculty of the Simon Fraser University Summer Publishing Workshops. In 2010, Richards's novel *Death Was in the Picture* won the Panik Award for best Los Angeles-based noir. Linda can be found at lindalrichards.com and @lindalrichards.

DISCOVER GAIL BOWEN'S CHARLIE D MYSTERIES

Charlie D is the host of a successful late-night radio call-in show, *The World According to Charlie D.* Each of these novels features a mystery that is played out in a race against time as Charlie D fights to save the innocent and redeem himself.

RAPID READS
WWW.RAPID-READS.COM